A Time To Awaken

Collected Art & Writings
of Ali Miner

An Ali Miner Book
Markowitz Publishing

Library of Congress Number 97-073090
ISBN 0-9655890-2-1

Ali Miner
Box Number 491, Pebble Beach, CA 93953
Phone: (408) 641-0845   Fax: (408) 641-0349

Distributed by Seven Hills Book Distributors
Printed in China through Palace Press International

Published by Markowitz Publishing
P. O. Box 1250, Paia, Hawaii 96779

The Birth of Consciousness Cards & Prints

Back in '93 with the help and encouragement of my husband, a few friends, lots of hard work, trial and error, 'Consciousness Cards' was born. The card line consists of many of the images and writings found in this book. The prints came along in '95. Since its creation, 'The Consciousness Line' has found its way across the United States and around the planet, bringing messages of love, hope and inspiration to many.

It has proven to be a powerful networking tool bringing hundreds of dynamic and wonderful new friends into my life! The response to my little company has been heartwarming and I sincerely express my thanks to all the wonderful friends, both known and unknown, who have bought my cards and prints and helped us grow and prosper so we can continue reaching out, touching hearts and helping to heal our precious little planet!

*Dedicated
to the unseen messengers and
guardians who lovingly accompany
and protect us every step
of our earthly sojourn and beyond…*

I wish to thank all the beautiful Angels who have so patiently awaited my own awakening and who have not given up on me; my beloved husband, Al McDaniel, without whose unwavering love, help and support I'd be totally lost and who, retired since 1986 still wants to know when the work stops and the fun begins; Gary Markowitz for his insistence on my proceeding with this project in the first place, his patience and tolerance of my moods and occasional doubts, and his wonderful talent in compiling all these 'images and wordscapes' and turning them all into a book…He's magic!…Aanjelae for her help, interest and enthusiasm for the book and Gary's devoted involvement with it…Alan Cohen, for providing this work a foreword that brought tears to my eyes when I first read it, and would have done so had it even been written for someone else. This is a man who writes from Divine Heart, who feels and touches us deeply, who illustrates so beautifully with the art of language that men possess Goddess energy too!…I am so honored…Thank you Alan!…My precious 'Loey'…Lois Larson, my great spiritual mentor and friend, without whom I might still be asleep. Loey gives so much to so many! She is, without a doubt, an angel in physical form; Loey's husband Ray, for his support and love and for allowing Loey to give so very much of herself to others; to dear Linda Hodes who looked at me, a Gilbert Williams book in her hand, and screamed, "You have to do a book!!!"…To all my precious friends for their encouragement and support, too many to name, but they all know I love them…And to Beloved Father-Mother God who has never let me down yet.

Sisters

Journey to the Center of the Heart

Forward

When I first set eyes upon Ali Miner's work, I had to stop what I was doing and just be with the image. I was touched by its simplicity, moved by its reverence, and inspired by its magnanimity. This gifted artist, I realized, had woven a magical synthesis of eloquence and heart. Who could ask for more?

Since I was seeking artwork for the cover of a meditation CD I was recording, *Journey to the Center of the Heart*, a light flashed above my head and I knew that Ali would be the perfect artist for the job. My intuition was confirmed when I contacted her and felt as if I had connected with a soul sister, a true kindred spirit. Ali went on to produce a magnificent work which you will find in this collection (facing page.)

You hold in your hands not simply a book of art, but an odyssey into the soul. There is no greater function of an artist than to remind us who we are, where we come from, and what we are capable of. Ali Miner does this, and more. She blends childhood innocence with divine romance to emerge with images that call forth cosmic memories of delight, beauty, and play. Her paintings titillate the imagination, thrill the senses, and nurture the spirit.

Here, as Ali gracefully marries art and verse, you will discover the breadth of her vision. She paints not simply to express herself, but as a cosmic wake-up call to refresh our knowingness of how we may love ourselves and each other more deeply, and how important is our role in the transformation of our world. We are not small, she demonstrates, but vastly grand. And within you is art as wondrous as the images you look upon; simply look within and you shall find your soul's gift.

I suggest that you use this book not simply for pleasure, but for meditation. Take an image and savor it, allowing the colors and forms to speak to your inner self. There are many messages here beyond the obvious. Each image is replete with divine symbols and loving essence. Ask, "What is the message here for me?" and quietly listen for a response from your inner guide. You shall receive. Then pore over the words not with your intellect, but with your heart. The same spirit that speaks through these images also speaks through the ideas formed by letters. Love has many languages, and we can hear them all if we are open.

My congratulations and blessings to Ali and publisher Gary Markowitz for their willingness to step forth and share this powerful work. We live in a world that so deeply needs beauty and upliftment. A gift like this is to be received with an open heart and mind, and shared. And if you should find inspiration here to remember your own greatness and express it, I know the artist and publisher would be deeply honored. I love Ali and I love her work; every time I look upon one of her pictures, I get lost in it — or, more accurately, I get found.

— Alan Cohen

Alan Cohen is the author of : *The Dragon Doesn't Live Here Anymore, I Had It All The Time.* Alan's monthly column *From the Heart* is syndicated in numerous magazines. Alan is also the Associate Editor of *New Frontier.*

Sisters

Sisters are we and will be to the end!
But more than a sister, you're my best friend!
When I'm hurting you listen...
And you soothe my heart.
Oh, please don't grow up and let us drift apart!
When I'm angry you calm me...
Make me smile when I'm blue
What would I ever do without you?
Oh, dearest sister, I just want you to know...
 "Heart to heart, toe to toe...
 A sister's love goes where you go!"

Journey to the Center of the Heart

A place so gentle, such love imparts...
We move now deeper in our hearts.
The shadows lift, pain is erased
We're healed, we're in a state of grace!
The wounded child no longer hurts...
She's free to love...He knows his worth!

We welcome you, Beloved Child...
To enter here and rest awhile.
Then open to the healing light
Of radiant beings who transform the night!

You're nurtured and loved here, right from the start
 In the great sacred temple
 At the center of the
 Heart

Little Mother's Angel

Our little cosmic homeland,
Our precious little planet,
A one-of-a-kind jewel you are...
Have we taken you for granted?
Should we re-assess our values; our goals;
Our priorities?
Have we been good stewards,
Conserved your resources,
Protected your atmosphere, your seas???
Oh dear, this is sad...
Please don't answer.
Sweet little angel takes you in her hands...
And to her heart.
She sends doves of peace to heal you
And prays mankind will start...
Being mindful of your needs,
 Our only Little Mother
 And bear in mind you're all we've got...
 There will not be another!

INTRODUCTION

It has often been said that artists see the world differently than others. Perhaps this is true. Given, we ALL see the world differently and from our own individual perspective, conditioned by upbringing, ethnic background, education, religious conviction, etc. The artist, however, is one who not only SEES things differently, but EXPRESSES things differently, thereby incurring the task of helping others see more clearly! He or she creates from visions seen with that 'inner eye'…perhaps from the soul. The artist 'sees' where other people see nothing, or see something entirely different! I don't believe artists 'become' artists, but are born artists. It's a sort of calling, a destiny. It's often an obsession known to have driven certain creative geniuses to the brink of madness. It is often a very lonely life and for some unrewarding during the span of their life, only to garner the prized recognition after that life is over. For others, fame, acclaim and even great wealth come during the current earthly sojourn and even early on. Whatever the case, one thing is certain: The artist must express that which burns within and yearns for expression. The artist must create!

I am thoroughly convinced that creativity is the key to our true spirituality; that living in the creative flow brings one nearer the Creator! We then and thereby become 'Co-Creators!' Just as *we* were created and all life we see around us was created by a great and powerful force, we, *as creations* must therefore possess a spark of that creative ability just as a tiny seed has within it the capability to become a mighty tree! We get to share in the Creator's creation process!

One does not HAVE to be an artist to create! Many people do not consider themselves very creative, yet they do creative things every day! Creativity can be applied to just about every facet of life! Creative living is an art form in itself.

It astounds me to hear someone say… "Oh, I'm not at *all* creative!"… Wow! What a put-down for the Creator! To think Mother-Father God would have short-changed you! I don't think so! This beautiful word, *Creativity*… the big 'C' word, is more important to you than you may realize! Your creativity is, to a great extent, who you are!

You are, first and foremost, a Beloved Child of God and I do hope you can accept that, because that is a great step toward knowing just how creative you truly are. The more you come to know the true divinity of your being and recognize it as a precious and sacred gift, the more you'll awaken to your unique, creative ability to express! How could a Beloved Child of such a sublime Creator be anything BUT creative! Ah! This is such an exciting thought! This is why I have created this book for you and for all my dear sisters and brothers, with paintings and messages created by my hand but with the help of angelic beings far wiser than myself who speak to me and whose presence is often very much felt just over my shoulder as I work. They have given me these images and messages to share with you to help bring you all forward into the light! The light of knowing who you are, how much you are loved, how precious you are and how much power you really do possess to bring about change in your own life and lives around you...

Knowing all this should definitely bring a lot of light into your life!

The title 'A Time To Awaken' was born of a long difficult labor. When finally settled upon, I and those dear ones working with me on the creation of this manuscript realized it simply couldn't be anything else! Why not? Because if ever there was a time on planet earth for us all to awaken, it is indeed now!

You may say... "But Man has always existed precariously and with great adversity! Great wars, grandiose atrocities, depravity, starvation, poverty, abuse, etc... So what's so different about today?"

The answer is simple. Technology is so advanced, the mechanisms of destruction are so lethal, we as a species have destroyed our environment to such an unimaginable extent, we are simply running out of time! Mother Earth will most likely survive our short, incompetent stewardship, however, we most likely will not!

How incomprehensible it is to think that a planet full of 'Beloved Children of God' let this happen! That's impossible! It must be someone else's fault!

Perhaps so many of us have simply forgotten who we really are and have fallen asleep...And as we sleepwalk through our daily, often discouraging lives, too busy struggling to survive and make ends meet we're missing the big picture! In our ignorance we punish poor old Mother Earth by inflicting every sort of pain and abuse imaginable upon her! I address this issue through the art and message of *The Crying Bird, Little Mother's Angel* and *Angel of the Seas* within the pages of this book.

Yes, this is indeed *A Time To Awaken!* And have you noticed of late the incredible advances in technology in the area of communication! Far too numerous to even hint upon here, but you know what I mean if you're a citizen of any modern or emerging country today. Never before in the history of the planet has communication been faster or more efficient, and yet, as far as I can see nobody seems to be listening to anybody! Everyone is too busy to listen! How ironic it all is! All these words fly through the wires and the waves, but who is listening? A minister's sermon I heard and yet remember from some years back contained the simple phrase:

"The first duty of Love is to listen!"

I think that's very important, don't you? Listening to one another has become a lost art!... To listen to someone is to honor them! It also makes you, the listener, feel better, as you have provided someone a service by being there for them! Good for your 'Karmic Bank Account!'

Husbands need to listen to wives; wives to husbands, men to women; women to men...and *all* of us need to listen to our children...

Do you suppose that awful habit kids have of not listening to their parents just might be acquired or learned behavior they picked up from us?...We'll give that one some thought...

Time to Awaken, boys and girls! There's work to be done! Awakening means stepping into the light of conscious living. Conscious living (*Consciousness*...the 2nd big "C" word) is thinking before acting, then acting for the highest possible good of everyone affected by our actions! In other words, creating a "win-win" situation. Seeing others as gifts and divine creations instead of competitors and adversaries. Treating one another with respect, as brothers and sisters instead of sex objects, cash cows, meal tickets, or untrustworthy strangers. Giving a hand to help and empower, not to weaken and enable, keeping in mind we do a disservice to others by doing for them what they should be doing for themselves. Far too many liberal viewpoints meant to bring about good have wrought destruction by taking away the divine individual incentive that is so precious to each and every developing human being! To be conscious is to be accountable for ones own actions, and when one lives by these guidelines, one is fulfilling their divine appointment! It has been said "Give a man a fish, feed him for a day, teach him to fish, feed him for a lifetime." Well and good! Then a friend added real polish to the old adage. He said: "Ah! but create a video on fishing and you can feed the whole world!"... Seems there's a high-tech twist to everything now-a-days!

In this age of intense consumerism and materialism it is often difficult to overcome desire for so many things. We are constantly bombarded by TV, radio, junk mail, E-mail, the web, billboards, salespeople, and on and on! Sometimes it becomes overwhelming! And often we give in, whip out the plastic or the checkbook, then feel guilty! Children are so vulnerable to this advertising frenzy that has taken control of our society! The "I wants" overtake us all at one time or another, but it's not always bad! As Beloved Children of God, we are entitled to 'goodies' now and then! However, when it becomes compulsion and obsession we must do the old reality check on ourselves, and regain control. Here is where creativity can come in very handy! Instead of being caught up on the 'accumulation' treadmill, how about a little more time spent on going within, enjoying who you are, your accomplishments, ways to express your uniqueness, perhaps studying something new and here-to-fore unexplored by you! Perhaps focus on someone who wronged you and with whom you are displeased. You have carried the burden of this resentment, even hatred for a time. It's a heavy burden and causes you pain inside, but you feel anger and just can't let it go! It's blocking your personal growth and you know you must let it go if you are to get on with your life. What would an Angel advise a Child of God to do about a situation like this? Do you suppose you might find forgiveness in your heart? You see, hatred and resentment are such boomerangs; they come back at you every time, but forgiveness is such a divine act you'll actually feel the wings sprouting on your shoulders! And what a rich deposit for that Karmic Bank Account... This one even pays a dividend! Good Karma and you get to dump a miserable burden, and most likely, the object of your grudge will never know how you feel, one way or the other! You forgive for YOU because of who YOU are, not who they are or what they did!

Turn off the barrage of media and external noise! Go stroll in the woods or on the beach, along a river, in a park and take the time to let the magnificence of nature infuse your being! Walk in the coolness of an evening or the dawn of a new day. Set aside some special time each day to nurture yourself and give thanks for the wonders of our beautiful world. Truly feel it, get into it, be a part of it! Learn to SEE, not just look, and know that all about you, this most magnificent creation was created just for you! After all, is a Beloved Child of God worthy of less? And it doesn't cost you anything! If you seek answers or need a miracle (and who doesn't from time to time?) just remember two things: First, the greatest miracle has already occurred... YOU ARE! ...Second, a thankful heart will CREATE the miracle you need! Just be patient and listen!

Women, my sisters, you possess the power to change the world! You are the mothers, the feminine energy, the nurturers, the healers. So much rests upon your shoulders! A number of the images and 'wordscapes' (As I like to call the writings!) in this book address this subject and the need for women to stand firm for their rights and the rights of women around the world. It matters not your background, your color, your beliefs or your lifestyle. Remember, you are a part of a sacred sisterhood, you are a giver of life, you are a Goddess! As a beautiful expression of the feminine energy you will heal our planet simply by seeing with eyes of love! Love will drive back the tide of evil and hatred, of greed, prejudice and fear as surely as light will drive away the darkness. Love is always the answer, whatever the question or situation! It's up to us to believe it and put it into practice, NOW! There's not a minute to waste!

Let us always keep in mind and heart the importance of children. Many images and wordscapes in this book address or are about children. Perhaps dearest to my heart is *The Healing* and *I Just Love You.* I hope they touch you at the deep level they were meant to. They touched me deeply during their creation process and they still do! *Angel of the Children* speaks to us profoundly as well. I'll say no more here, but invite you to delve into the following pages of *A Time To Awaken* and experience these divinely inspired messages for yourself. May your journey be uplifting, inspiring and fulfilling. If your heart is touched as you view and read, if you find a ray of hope where perhaps you were experiencing despair, if you find renewed faith in yourself and your own unique God-given potential, the Universe and a new tomorrow, then the Angels will be pleased and perhaps they will permit me to work with them on future projects!

— Ali

Little Mother's Angel

A Time To Awaken

Collected Art & Writings
of Ali Miner

Bringers of the Dawn

Oh, night please fly, be done with you!

Be through and gone away!

Come!...Oh Bringers of the Dawn

Make me a brand new day!

Bring me the light in radiant hues...

Bring fire from heavenly places.

Oh, drive back the night, the pain and the fright

With the hope that a new dawn embraces!

Oh, call, Gentle Spirits of Light and of Dawn...

Whisper to us to awaken.

As your angelic faces appear in pink clouds

To assure us we've not been forsaken!

*Front Cover Image

Bringers of the Dawn

The Visitation

While sitting in quiet contemplation
An Angel came through meditation.
Surprised was I and asked "Are you real?"
I reached forth my hands so Her gown I might feel.
I touched only air where she seemed to be...
So I thought I was dreaming this Angel by me!
My hands still outstretched, they seemed frozen that way
Then suddenly they held an enormous bouquet!

"A gift just to say that we hear your prayers
To inform you God listens and to tell you God cares!
To let you know God answers...Do you want to know how?...
In the silence, In the silence.
To let you know you're loved beyond what words convey,
To tell you you're protected every night and every day!
When you're in need of answers, there's really just one way...
In the silence, In the silence.
My child, you have power beyond what you know!
It's God's greatest pleasure to grandly bestow
All that you wish and all that you need
You have only to ask, you need only believe!
When asking, go inward...prepare to receive...
In the silence, In the silence.

This visitation is concluded and one more thought I add
That listening surpasses whatever you might ask
So often prayers are answered...
But our ears are closed to God!
For the noise we make is far too great
So we think that He forgot!

Our answers always come, Remember what I said
Listen, my child and you will know...
Here's how, where, why and when...
In the silence, In the silence."

The Visitation

Angel of Creativity

She nurtures the creative spirit in little angels
And in us all!
She reminds us we are all creative beings . . .
Each with special and unique gifts to share.
She encourages the children to explore their magical,
Creative natures.
This is how they learn self worth.
She invites us all to accept this challenge of introspection
And self discovery . . .
For this is how we experience fulfillment
And discover our true identity.
Expression of creativity is our divine birthright,
The manifestation of our unlimited potential
Limit not thyself!

As Beloved Children of God,
We are all vital parts of Creation . . .
Perfect, precious, unlike any other!
Creativity is true spirituality,
Therefore, the very essence of our being!
Embrace joyfully your uniqueness.
Take delight in the wonderful, creative being that is
Exclusively
You!

Angel of Creativity

Angels of Inner Peace

Come be beside us…Come fill our hearts

With peace and serenity your presence imparts.

Tell us, Our Angels, that we can let go…

And share in this peace

That we're longing to know.

Say it's alright to join in the dance…

To lay down these burdens

That keep us entranced.

Thinking that struggle is the way to survive,

That we need to feel pain to know we're alive!

Whisper gently to us that we might be serene…

We wait to fly away with you

To places we've but dreamed!

Angels of Inner Peace

♥ I Just Love You ♥

I Just love you, it's as simple as that!

No conditions, no strings, that's just where it's at!

I see in you beauty, I see in you love,

I see you in white light, you're God's Precious Dove!

I vibrate to your laughter, I hurt at your pain

When you cry I just pray 'till you smile once again!

To have you in my life has given so much

That words are inadequate to express such.

I see you as perfect in all that you do...

You're God's Beloved Child...

And I just love you!

I Just Love You

Mists of Dawn

How can one witness a scene such as this
And doubt the presence, the power, the profound Love
Of infinite mind, The Creator?
These are reflected in every sunrise, every sunset,
Every flower, every tree...
In each and every feather
Of every bird that has ever flown...
Every wave that ever washed upon any shore...
The face of every child,
The beauty of every animal,
The heart of every man and every woman...
I am in awe!!!

Mists of Dawn

Gentle Spirit...
Child of Light!...

Thoughts of you are my heart's delight!
Walk with grace in your gown of white,
 Go softly on the earth.

Keep light your heart, be free to love
Reach forth your hand... caress the dove
Be at peace with yourself
And the Angels above
 And go lightly on the earth.

Little lady of the lake
A world of magic you create...
So sweet a child, so pure and true
The birds rush in and flock to you!
So will it be for all mankind...
When hearts are healed and eyes aren't blind
Can we see far enough to know what we'll find...
 If we go consciously on the earth?

When we grow and gentle spirits be...
Through loving thoughts and honesty
All our needs will well be met,
Kind hearts attract good; fear creates lack!
Abundance for each and every man
As when Creator conceived the plan.
Doves flock fearlessly to every hand...
 We'll all go gently on the earth.

Gentle Spirit

Evening Meditation—

He Leadeth Me Beside the Still Waters . . .

He restoreth my soul:

He leadeth me in the paths of righteousness

for His name's sake.

Yea, though I walk through the valley

of the shadow of death,

I will fear no evil for Thou art with me.

Thy rod and thy staff they comfort me.

Thou preparest a table before me

in the presence of mine enemies;

Thou anointest my head with oil; my cup runneth over.

Surely goodness and mercy shall follow me

all the days of my life . . .

And I will dwell in the house of the Lord forever.

The 23rd Psalm

Evening Meditation

Goddess and Children
in
Mr. Monet's Garden

Sweet Angel... play your sweet song for the children; abide awhile where he walked and loved nature. He spoke to the flowers and trees, and they to him. They came to life under his artist's eye...they danced for him. He in turn immortalized them on his magic canvases. He drew from his garden, this slice of heaven on earth, a creative energy that can only come from the bosom of Mother Earth. He understood well his relationship to and with Her.

He watches from the bridge, his loving eye overseeing the unfolding, enchanting scene, as children awaken to the creative energy that so deeply inspired him while in this life!

He beckons them to tap into the abundant reservoir of inspiration his garden yet imparts. He listens dreamily as the notes from the Goddess's harp float across his pond and gently touch his ear. He will never leave the garden. Papa Monet will always be a magical part of his magical garden and both Goddess and children will _always_ be welcome!

Goddess & Children in Mr. Monet's Garden

A Basket Full of Flowers

My child what brings you to this garden,

You're a long way from home…

Have you come all this way

And spent most of your day

But through this thicket to roam?

It seems you must truly love flowers

To gather so tenaciously,

Or perhaps you love one who loves flowers more…

And you gather for him, not for thee.

If in fact you do pick for another,

Perhaps someone aged or ill,

A grandma, a friend, someone saddened or down,

Then you truly are doing God's Will!

For flowers are God's way of giving,

A gift that speaks truly of love!

And like love, must be shared

For to gather and keep

Is simply not good enough!

A Basket Full of Flowers

Homecoming

The world is a dreamscape that exists in the mind of the artist and the child...
A world of enchantment that fades off to infinity...
Where day and night are but one, where always the Goddess's song may be heard and the air is pure and clean!

The crystal mountain possesses 'All Wisdom of All Ages.'
The children run joyously there to be taught by 'Enlightened Ones' of the Crystalline Realm...
Beyond all they will be taught and all wisdom they will acquire there, the greatest and most important lesson they will learn and carry within throughout life's journey will be...

"Love for oneself and for one another...
Acknowledgement of our eternal oneness with God and all Life, respect for Mother Earth, for Truth, and for All Creation provides us the freedom to know and experience our true 'Homecoming'...whereby we are always 'at home' and 'at peace,' each and every one of us, within our own being, no matter where life takes us, or what our circumstances!"

We are all 'Beloved Children of God!'

Homecoming

Guardian Angel in Training

Now, my little Angel, I will teach you all I know...

Your training has begun so please...Listen as we go!

Out there the vastest universe...of galaxies and space

Below a planet known as 'Earth'...A truly wondrous place!

Never has been seen since God first made the plan

A sphere of such majestic beauty...

Or a more curious creature than 'Man!'

The animals need not our care; they understand the scheme

They live in peace and harmony and fulfill the Maker's dream!

They do not war and desecrate, destroy, pollute and hate...

But 'Man!'...This strange dichotomous beast!

What will be his fate???

Beware my little Angel! Your task is great, I know!

It almost seems too late for them and planet earth below...

But still, you must be vigilant and touch their hearts and minds...

And plant your seeds of Love and Truth

And strive to save Mankind!

Guardian Angel in Training

Angel of the Seas

Angel of the seas, protector of the creatures...
In light you come, they know you well
They all join in to greet you!
They need to speak and share with you
Their heart-felt deep concern,
They understand the urgency that invokes your return.

They see their home so deep and blue, their sacred sanctuary
Is being used as a garbage dump 'n it's gettin' mighty scary!!
Beer cans float by, bottles, papers 'n such, tons of plastics 'n
All kinds of junk!
The oil tankers think of the sea as a place
To dump their gooey black gunk!
These creatures know man's nets and harpoons
Mean death to themselves and their young...
Everything down there, edible or not, must get out of man's way...
Or they're sunk!
"What can we do?" Asks the manatee sadly...
And the dolphins echo his plea...
The whales cry their long and mournful call for Man-Brother
To wake up and see!
The seas are not infinite; can't forever self-cleanse
Sooner or later must cease...
This mindless destruction of our deep blue realm...
Man's awareness must quickly increase!
"I Know!" Says the Humpback..."I have a plan!
We'll call on the children, 'cause they'll understand!
Young humans are open and know of our plight...
They're ready to help us in this noble fight!
They'll teach the old ones to open their eyes,
To stop desecrating US, our earth, seas and skies!
To protect a heritage in which we all share,
Maintain the vigil and learn how to care.
For it's the children's future...They hold the key!
And if they do not respect this...we'll all cease to be!!"

Angel of the Seas

Angel of Divine Flow

Life is now, life is ever
Life abounds, ceasing never!
Love is now, lives in our hearts
It never stops, it never starts!
It always was, will always be
The 'Divine Flow' in all we see!
The value of life is life itself,
The love in your heart is your true
Wealth!

The miracle has occurred...
...You Are!
Celebrate!!!

Angel of Divine Flow

Angel of Non-Judgement

She sees with her heart, _not_ her eyes...
She Judges _not_!
The world below awakens as the children reach, hungering
Toward the light that bridges all differences, prejudices,
Misunderstanding.
Tired of conflict, tired of judgement,
Ready to accept one another on equal terms;
To embrace, to love, to work together!

The tree of life is formed of human branches...
Each an integral part...
This tree will bear all the fruit of an
       Abundant harvest!

Seeing with our hearts more and our eyes and egos less,
Our differences become shadowy impostors; unimportant!
Our 'samenesses' become more apparent...
We now enter the illumination of knowing...

      We are all one!

Angel of Non-Judgement

43

♥

'Tis **Not**
How
Big the
Dream...
But
How Great
The Faith
and
Determined
the
Heart!

♥

No Dream Too Great

...No star too high !
No goal too big...Shoot for the sky !
Let no one tell you you can't have your dream...
Let no one sell you on some lesser scheme !
Hold faith in yourself and the universe too...
When your heart is decided
No door is closed to you !
No one can stop you or stand in your way,
The angels will guide you on your path...
Day by day !
Remember Who you are, then,
The birthright you possess...
A Beloved Child of God you are !
Never see yourself as less !

No Dream Too Great

Angel of Motherhood

Blessed is each and every child who has come onto this earth...

Blessed is each mother who has given each child birth.

Blessed the work of many years to raise up each little one...

That one day each mother may feel deeply proud

Of her own special daughter or son.

And one day the Angel of Motherhood

Will come to you gently to say...

 "Yes, the hours were long, the pay often poor

 But yours was a job most well done!

 I Know, for you see...I was there all the time

 Aware of your joy and your pain...

 I come now to tell you how much you are loved...

 That nothing you did was in vain!

 You're a light to the world for all that you give

 And I'll be by your side for as long as you live!"

 Blessed be!

Angel of Motherhood

Garden of Innocence

A 'wordscape' for this painting had not come through. This A.M. it was revealed to me _why_! It was not to be a poem...I was not to write _about_ 'Garden of Innocence,' but was to be a participant _in_ it!

I was doing my usual workout above Carmel Beach this lovely June Sunday morning, (Both Carmel Beach and Sundays are magical, thus, anything can happen!) a series of stretching and twisting I do with a 5 ft. long pole...when suddenly 3 sandy-haired youngsters burst through the thicket and flopped down nearby...2 boys and a girl, and all bore earmarks of Huck Finn..."Watcha practicin' for?" one asked. I laughed and told him I was exercising..."Oh, neat!" A flood of questions ensued. The boys, 7 and 9 were brothers; the girl, 8, their cousin. They shared many things with me in the following few minutes, including a rather remarkable demonstration of backflips that almost cost Kyle, the youngest, a broken neck and me a coronary... Kenny, the senior proudly rolled up pants legs to reveal an impressive collection of abrasions, bruises and scars; Kyle, not to be outdone (and he wasn't) did likewise! Battle scars, proudly earned! Joy, not quite as eager for 1st place, but not to be left out, shared her token collection of bumps and bruises; much milder, thank heaven! They expressed with great exuberance their love for somersaulting and rolling down the enormous sand dunes, climbing atop the roof of the public restrooms, getting filthy dirty and generally living life to its lustiest, fullest measure! I found myself, next I knew, careening down the huge dune along with them, all four of us laughing, racing, yelling and jubilant! I loved these three vibrant little pure souls; what's more, I was one of them...for these few moments. I knew it, and so did they. We were all equals, we were all joy filled children! How appropriate the little girl was named Joy! I continued on, swinging my pole, stretching my limbs, the kids skipping and chattering at my side, so full of life, so free..."Hey, let's go look for golf balls...wanna come, Ali?" I replied I'd watch them as I continued my routine from the shoreline, and bid them 'good luck.' They ran back toward the steep, grassy incline that separates Carmel beach from Pebble Beach Golf Course. I watched them comb for balls in the tall soft grass of the hill, dashing about, then rolling down the undulating grass. They waved and hollered to me, I to them...They ran down to me once more, then darted off in pursuit of another wild adventure.

These children made this morning so special...they let me be; _made_ me be, a child along with them, unquestioningly, and live totally in the _NOW_ of the moment! What a great lesson! They taught me the importance of sustaining wounds when going for the gusto of the great bounty life has to offer; of living your dreams...without fear!

Thank you my little teachers, Kyle, Kenny and Joy, for your beautiful lesson and permitting me to be a child with you today in the 'Garden of Innocence.'

I pray all children may share in your joy and freedom to express, and we 'older' children might learn to appreciate and value this great gift you have to share with us.

Garden of Innocence

Divine Decision

She holds a ball of fire, he presents a heart of love
A reasonable solution for an Angel from above.
But the matriarch is wiser and she knows all too well
This heart is not enough to change what's in this 'ball of hell.'
This ball is war and hate and greed and all that's evil in Man...
And time has come to take it out and resume a peaceful plan.
Give Her back to the stewards who do not war...
Who in peace respect the earth.
Give Her back to the animals, great and small,
So our Mother may have a rebirth.
Take Her out of the hands of the evil ones
Who care _not_ what they do!
Those who follow a path of destruction and hate...
The time has come to review!
And the Angels pray for the hearts of men, even the evil ones
That they might awaken and someday perceive
That they too were daughters and sons.
That the earth was theirs too, to love and protect
And their brothers and sisters likewise.
But instead they chose hate, thus it was too late!
Their tenure was compromised!
A new dawn! The innocents rise up and rejoice in harmony!
These peaceful souls whose gentle ways allow them to be free
To love the earth, respect her well and use her responsibly.
And the Angels smile toward the gentle ones
Who nurture both land and sea,
Those who honor _all_ life, bear burden and strife
To save earth for posterity!

Divine Decision

Angel of the Lovers

A special place for lovers…The Angels know it well!
It's far removed from mundane things;
It's where the Angels dwell!
They're drawn there by your whispers…
You, who speak with hearts and eyes,
You, whose love for each other brings heaven to earth
And makes earth seem a part of the skies!
Being in love is transforming; gives greater reason to live.
Being in love is adoring, sharing dreams, learning to
Give!
Oh, how could the Angels not be there?
Each one assigned to two hearts,
How could they not want to join in
The uniting as one of two parts!
Tell me, what more could an Angel ask
Than to watch over two souls in love?
Does not love replace fear?
Is there something more dear?
Is it not sent from heaven above?
Please remember to cherish each other
Please remember how precious love is!
Help your Angel to guide you and protect your love well
By loving each other
As long as you live!

Angel of the Lovers

High Tea

What do Angels talk about when they pause to take 'High Tea?'

Do they talk about the earth plane and mortals like you and me?

Do they discuss heavenly politics or life-forms on planets afar?

Or do they simply speak of love and subjects of the heart?

Perhaps it's culture, philosophy, music and literature,

Perhaps man's varied religions, and how they're

All so very sure

That their way is the only one,

Be they worshipping saviors, gold calves or the sun!!

Or perhaps they simply sip and pray...

That we might All sit together...

And share

'High Tea'

Someday!

High Tea

Guardian Angel

You're never alone... Just reach out your hand

I'm your Guardian Angel and I'll understand.

I'm here to help you when all else seems lost

I'm here to support you

As on life's seas you're tossed.

I am your guardian, I hear your call...

Not a thing you can't share with me...

Not too big or too small!

I bless you with comfort, understanding and hope,

Yes, I know when you're tired

And at the end of your rope.

I know when your heart is breaking in two...

This doesn't deter me...I'll still stand by you!

For this is my job here; for this I was sent!

I'll see you through 'till this life on earth's spent.

And I'll be there after, as your travels progress,

Still reaching out to you, I'll love you no less!

You're my Beloved...

It's you that I bless!

Guardian Angel

Angel of Creation

Oh, Angel fair, earth's oceans pure
From your hands cascade down.
You carry the animals great and small
In the folds of your ethereal gown.
I see the land as if it flowed
Directly from your heart,
Now could it be that this is how it

Really all did start ???

Forget 'Big Bang' and scientists
Who try to reason with logic...
Let's look at the spiritual, the purely metaphysical...
Now I find it all quite ironic!
How creatures on earth share love and give birth,
They rear and they nurture their young.
    'Big Bang' can't 'splain that
    T'was an Angel by drat!
That's how it all was begun!

Angel of Creation

Angel of the Plains

This vast expanse of land, Oh, Great and Mighty One
You gave to us so we might go watch
Rivers and wild horses run!
You gave to us a space so wide, a sky of limitless scope.
A place to be apart from stress
And bring to our hearts a new hope!
A place where we might be set free...
To connect with the meaning of life...
Where buffalo thundered, Indian hunted
And Great Spirit took "Wind" for His wife.

Now the eagle swoops down; his eyes flash with life...
He screams as he dodges a crow,
He cries, "This is my land...I came before man,
My extinction he's bound to bestow!"
Oh, the wild horses run, and the rivers do too
Not as many now as once there were...
Great Buffalo's thunder is no longer heard...and we ask,
"Will he ever return?"
Then all at once, an Angel appears...
He hovers over the land...
Oh! He's blessing it, loving it, sending down light
From the very palms of his hands!
He's blessing me too and I'm filled now with hope...
As he shares the reason he's here
"I'm the Angel of the Plains," he affirms...
"My Father requests I appear...
To protect sacred lands that are precious to me...
And those creatures to soon disappear."

My heart fills with joy that he's chosen to come!...
And suddenly... I...
And Great Spirit
Are One!

Angel of the Plains

We will
pray both night and
day
That peace on
earth will
come
to stay ...
That children
here
and children
there
might be well fed
and
Not know
fear ...

That wars
 will stop,
compassion
start...
and
Love
 will come
to every
heart! ...

This we pray!

Angel of the Children

When 'Angel of the Children' was presented to
me as a vision, as do come most of my paintings,
she came as a mime-like lady, and I knew that
was exactly how she was to be depicted,
though I knew then not why ...
As I was adding the finishing touches, I was
visited by a friend; a gentle, angelic person
herself...and very perceptive.
As she observed the painting a sort of
knowingness came over her kind face,
and she said in the softest voice...
     "Oh! But of course you painted
'Angel of the Children' to resemble a mime!" ...

"Why do you say so?" I asked, surprised at her
keen perception, having made no prior mention to
her of this odd resemblance.
"But, don't you know?" she queried,
herself now surprised.
"No," I replied, "I really don't! She just came
to me that way! ... Do you know why?"
     She replied ...
     "Because the children have no
          voice."

Angel of the Children

Angel of the Rain Forest

Here is an Angel whose work is so great,
She knows her domain holds the key to our fate!
The planet entire has need of her trees,
Yet 'Greed' cuts them down for his own selfish needs!
Then there are others who in ignorance chop . . .
They cut, slash and burn...
Oh! When will it stop??!!
They clear off the land, burn all the trees,
So there go the critters
Who live up in the leaves!
Their homes will be gone, their food source will too,
As our rainforests vanish, extinctions ensue!
Mother Earth sees this danger drawing ever more near,
She calls on us all to wake up and hear!

    She says:

      "Open your eyes now, before it's all gone!
You must help protect Me! . . . This destruction is wrong!
You can't cut my forests and burn all my trees
Then leave my poor creatures to starvation . . . disease!
This is not conscientious you <u>will</u> pay a <u>price</u>!
I fear for you, children . . . It will not be nice!

    You best clean your act up, accountable be...
    And take care of your Mother . . . If a future you'll see!
    You best help my Angel in her noble fight
    For we all need these forests . . .

      Just as darkness needs light!"

Angel of the Rain Forest

Ribbons from a Goddess's Hair

The Creator is a Goddess…I'll tell you how I know!
I see the world as ribbons, straight from Her hair they flow!
Each ribbon tumbles down from Her… So long it has no end
As it unfurls and twists and curls
Appear the gifts that She doth send.
Some ribbons become rivers,
They wind through rocks and fields,
Some spiral down and in their folds
Are dolphins, whales and seals!

There are swans and doves, flowers and trees,
People embracing or racing on skis!
There are children chasing butterflies,
Cockatoos, pelicans, beaches and skies…
There are rainforests, mountains, rainbows and falls,
There are oceans of fishes…I can't name them all!

Polar bears, penguins, pandas and cranes,
How does She remember so many names?
How can these ribbons so magical be?!
I am just awe-struck by all that I see!
Thank you, Mother Goddess,
For these gifts you've given me!

Ribbons from a Goddess's Hair

In the Beginning...

...The Goddess held forth her hands...
Pools of Liquid Crystal appeared...

And as she gazed lovingly on and breathed gently out,
There appeared life forms...
They jumped and played in the pools of her palms!
Then the liquid crystal cascaded down
And the seas were formed
The creatures frolicked and multiplied and the Goddess
Was exceedingly happy...

And thus it _all_ began!

Let us never forget the sacredness of
Creation!!

In the Beginning

The Awakening
Lovely Goddess...Behold Thyself!

In your awakening and transcendence you are admired, loved and desired, but you hold firmly the key to your destiny...Somehow the destiny of the world rests with you...You are a Goddess in the chrysalis! The time has come to understand your femininity and the power you possess! Your form may appear delicate but your power can subdue the world, once trained and focused as the Goddess! You need not physical strength. Your strength lies within your heart, mind and soul! You need only to awaken to claim it! Nurture well your dreams, fantasies and creativity...they are essential to your strength and the essence of who you are! Be proud of this. Give your creativity free reign to play a part in creating change and a better world!

Reach out and teach others to grow and walk in light. Accept your birthright; claim it now! But remember... All will be lost if you choose to sleepwalk on your journey and fail to recognize the Goddess in those very eyes looking back from your own looking glass!

The Awakening

Return of the Goddess

Arise, O Goddess, in glory and pride!

We now claim our power

And shall not leave your side!

Sisters unite, for *now* is the time!

So many do suffer, so many are blind!

Oh Goddess, please lead us, please show us the way!

For together we're strong and empowered we'll stay!

Old masculine mindsets be met with disdain,

The Goddess returns with her feminine reign.

A time now for love, for compassion and giving.

From the heart, and in spirit

Will we all begin living!

Return of the Goddess

The Crying Bird

She elegantly graces her great white steed streaming through the galaxies, flocks of great white birds soaring at her sides. They flee 'Old' Mother Earth, she, carrying in the waves of her ocean-like hair and fertile matrix-gown all the elements of life-forms of Beloved Mother Earth she is able, a veritable 'Noah's Ark' galloping among the stars, distancing herself from the final destruction occurring back on precious Old Mother Earth...There is great sadness. The great white bird weeps as she looks back; the great horse weeps as he forges onward and upward.

The children afore and aft represent male and female energy...She holds him uncertainly, her eyes ask... "Will he grow up to pursue war and aggression as so many generations of men before him on Old Mother Earth or will he be an enlightened one unto a new age of peace-loving men on 'New' Mother Earth?"...She ponders...

For she loved Mother Earth so! She was the Mother Goddess, the Guardian of Sacred Life who breathed love, joy, beauty and laughter into all hearts, who, in union with The Creator blessed all creation. She looks back knowing it didn't have to be so! If only her children had awakened in time! Old Mother Earth was not ready to die, but alas, she took the abuse as long as she could before she breathed her last! She gave of her seas, her lands, her air, and gave and gave, but man just took and took and destroyed, polluted and killed...

The birds carry twigs in their beaks to begin construction on New Mother Earth awaiting them, shining bright in the distance, so unknown and unexplored! Will there be trees for their nests?

'The Crying Bird' was the first of my transitional pieces, marking the beginning of my journey into the realm of visionary-spiritual message art. It is symbolic, of course, but the message is most pertinent for us all.

Dying 'Old' Mother Earth represents old mindsets, old ego-greed-fear-power-based ways of thinking that will always, eventually and inevitably lead to destruction. The shining new planet represents the awakened, enlightened consciousness. All the migrating creatures represent our potential, soaring upward to new heights, new possibilities, beyond old limited ways of thinking. Finally, this is a painting about hope. 'New' Mother represents hope! We can save our planet and ourselves, but not through lethargy and denial. We must work without ceasing to clean up our environment, turn away from aggression, prejudices, hatred, fear, negative addictions and excuses, and open our hearts and minds to love, keeping in mind at all times, our oneness with all creation!

The Crying Bird

The Healing

Oh, Beloved Child...you're not really alone
Though your path has been long
And your pain was unknown...
There's an Angel who's with you...
She came 'cause she knew
That you needed a friend...
Someone there...Just for you!
She brings hope and comfort, magic and love
She calls in the animals from land, sea and
Above!
The dolphins will rise up, the mammals caress
For they cry when they see a child in distress!
Their kind hearts are heavy
Great sadness they'll feel...

Until that great day when the
Last Child Can Heal!!!

'The Healing' was painted for a little girl named Faith, my niece, in the hope it will someday help her to heal the many emotional scars from years of abuse. It is my sincere hope it will help others to heal as well.

The Healing

We're Having Fun Now!

When Life's many problems get you down,
Don't get hung up on it, go clown around!!
Take '5,' take time out, regroup, meditate...
Just go have some fun before it's too late!!
Go swimming, go running, take a walk, catch a show...
Be like the critters here, let your hair down,
                    Let Go!!

Go out into nature, pet a tree, kiss a bear,
Go slide down a mountain, go laugh in the mirror!
Go find someone lower and cheer up their day!
Tell someone you love them...then for heaven's sake,
                    Go Play!!

We're Having Fun Now!

Celestial Waters

Angels pour, a siren sings,
The waters are alive with beings!
She strokes her harp...It sounds so sweet
A world of joy where innocents meet!
A world where all the children heal,
As they frolic with dolphins, turtles and seals.
A world where pain does not exist...
A world where they are truly blessed!
By Celestial Waters,
By a siren's song...
This deep sense of knowing
It's here they belong!
A scene of such amazing grace,
There's so much love, there's so much space!
There's joy beyond imagining...
In the exhilaration of just simply being!
Of merging with creatures who live in the wild,
What a beautiful vision...dolphin and child!
They're all so precious...we love them all so
Let's nurture and protect them
So they're free
To live and grow!

Celestial Waters

Hide and Seek

Hide yourself among the trees
He plays so sweetly...yet you tease
His one desire, you to please
    And yet you run away!
You hide from him, or think you do...
But do you hide from him...or you?
You once were hurt so said..."No more!!
My heart I'll keep forever more!"
I'll lock away my love inside,
Behind the trees I'll run and hide
For surely hearts don't have to cry...
    If you let them run away!
His heart hurts too, for you he loves...
He'd give you the moon and the heavens above!
The stars as well if it would be enough...
    To make you stop running away!
A heart that won't give love a chance
Is a heart that will never learn to dance.
So when in life love comes your way
    Don't run and hide, don't run away!
Perhaps it's the answer to your deepest prayer
Someone has come who really does care!
But your fear says "No...It cannot be!
    I'll just keep running away!
My heart is locked in yonder fortress
Huge doors and walls of stone repress
What thoughts I have to seek a love...
    I _must_ keep running away!"
Then suddenly an Angel comes
To touch your heart and heal your wounds...

Though from love you do run, God's not left you forsaken
He speaks to your heart...It's time to awaken!
God's sacred gift to the entire earth
Is the love that joins couples and gives children birth!
A heart filled with love is what gives us self worth...
    Not playing 'Hide and go seek!'
How many wish love would come their way?
Yet desperately suffer through each lonely day.
Praying for someone to come and to say...
    "You don't have to run any more!"

Hide & Seek

Arise!

Arise child, my fair one, step into your dream.
Your world is a dreamscape and not what it seemed.
Some say you're a dreamer and well you might be!
But they're locked in illusion of what their eyes see.

When others see anger, you see only love
When others see difference, you see us as one
When others are jealous, you praise openly
You encourage us all to be all we can be!

You see with your heart first, set judgement aside
In each one you meet you see Christ in their eyes.
You touch us so gently, an Angel are you . . .
For the goodness you share
And the love that shines through!

. . . One day we'll all hold your vision
And step into your dreamscape with you!

Arise!

Beloved

Magic abounds!

My heart leaps at the thought of

My beloved.

The face of love appears everywhere...

And love appears in every face.

The world seems gentler,

The sun brighter,

The air fresher...

And I, more aware of it All!

...More Alive!

Suddenly, words of songs were written just for you...

Gardens grow where fallow fields were but yesterday.

Butterflies appear from nowhere

And when did the birds learn to sing So sweetly?

Angels envelop us in ribbons of rainbow light...

You have opened my heart

And filled it

With love...

Beloved

Song of Meditation

So quiet is my special place...
So far from all distraction
And there I go to sit and pray
And lose myself in meditation.
As I sit so still, a dove appears
And lights upon my hand.
The ocean rolls, the breezes blow,
And gently the leaves begin to chant.
The birds join in...They chirp and sing,
The doves do gently coo...
A cricket, a frog, some creatures unknown
An owl with his mournful "whoooo"

These sounds of the living forest
Are my relaxation chorus!
It's my 'Song of Meditation'...
It's God's loving and gentle vibration.

Song of Meditation

Higher Self-The Child Revealed

A story of unfoldment...And then you reach a place
Where the layers peel back one by one...
And you're confronted with a face!

A face so small, a face of light, of innocence so pure...
A child it is!
Then something deep within you starts to stir.
You know this child...Your heart takes flight,
You've touched upon a truth!

This child is *you* from long ago...
Before the adult claimed the youth.

You see him jump and laugh and play
With heart so light and smile so bright.
You see her run through fields that sway
With flowers of a distant yeserday.
He reaches out; She's ready now...
To help you heal and grow,
This little child who lives in you...
Your Higher Self to know!

Higher Self - The Child Revealed

Gifts of Love

Gifts of Love . . .
Are not bought and are not given
But flow freely
From heart to heart ♥▸♥

Ali —
The Artist-The Author

Childhood was neither fun nor happy so I did everything in my power to become an adult as quickly as possible. Only when I actually reached the status of 'adult'... (if indeed I have!) did I feel comfortable enough with myself to begin enjoying childhood and the things of childhood. As a small person I was just too vulnerable to the painful experiences I encountered to actually enjoy being a child. My only comfort was my darling, doting grandmother who adored me almost to the embarrassing exclusion of every other child in the entire family! She was my first Angel! God has sent me many throughout my life!

Born in Mt. Vernon, New York, April 3rd 1949, the first of four, I grew up there until age twelve, then in the unexciting suburb of Hazlet, New Jersey, where my parents decided to move in order to capture their small share of the American Dream.

We left the big old 165 family apartment building, my only home since birth, and moved to our utopia-of-the-60s tract-house dream in the middle of nowhere. I hated it at first but adjusted as I made new friends. An artistic child since my earliest memory, always sketching in pencil and pastels, I had my first set of oils at age 12 when my grammar school teacher recommended to my parents I be enrolled in adult night school art classes at the local high school. I felt terribly intimidated, both by the oils and the older people in the class. I didn't stay too long, but did stay with the oils... now over 35 years and still loving them! I occasionally work in other mediums, have actually worked in many, but prefer oils over everything else. I have painted everything from the faces of tiny pocket watches to enormous set designs for stage plays. My work has been used or

93

commissioned for magazines, books, CDs and tapes, portraiture, murals, menus, and catalogs. I have sold hundreds of paintings and thousands of prints that hang in collections around the world.

Angels and Goddesses began appearing on my canvases in 1989 when my beautiful Angel-friend / spiritual mentor, Lois, shared her botanical potion, KM, with me, which she at the time thought was quite the magical tonic (and still does!) It tasted terrible, but she insisted I keep taking it. So, for her, I'd do anything... I kept taking it! Weeks passed... nothing... Then one day, with a jolt I realized I hadn't had one depressed moment in weeks! I had been prone to frequent depression throughout my life so this was truly a miracle! Could it be the KM? Then my art totally changed! I began having visions and in came Angels and Goddesses, etc. Prior to that my work was very different and did NOT contain Angels or Goddesses. I knew it was definitely the KM! I take it to this day, and have never had a recurrence of depression.

Another dear Angel-friend, around 1992 suggested I begin creating writings (word pictures or word-scapes) to go with my paintings, so I did! Shortly thereafter, my 'Consciousness Cards' line was born.

At age 15, a near drowning experience would have well retired me from this particular earthly sojourn, had I not heard 'THE VOICE' say to me, as I languished on the ocean floor, pommeled by huge waves and being beckoned into a beautiful, dry, brilliantly lit tunnel of pure white light, "GO UP! YOU'RE NOT READY YET!" I obeyed, and not a second too soon! I reached the surface gasping, and realizing what had just almost happened, but had no time to ponder it as the waves were relentless, and I was so far out I could hardly see land. It was the Jersey Shore and there was a storm out at sea. I had no business swimming that day, especially alone! But I was 15, fearless, indestructible and adored the ocean. Now I was totally alone, terrified, and feeling pretty powerless in the face of this mighty, raging ocean all around me! I forgot about 'THE VOICE' and the "YOU'RE NOT READY YET" part, or surely thought HE forgot about me! Then, low and behold, not too far off to my left, another insane swimmer! Oh, my God, I thought, and screamed "HELP" as loudly as I could over the din of erratically crashing waves and howling wind. My only companion was a wicked undertow dragging me farther and farther from the direction in which I was trying so desperately to swim in the deep, murky water. The unknown swimmer heard my cry, took it seriously and was at my side quicker than seemed humanly possible. He took my hand and asked, "Do you know how to tumble?" To which I gasped "No, only body-surf." (Remember now, this was in the days before boogie boards!) ... OK. No time to waste here... "Do what I do... Follow me!" He commanded... Rolling himself in a ball, with each wave he rolled, forward instead of backward, as I had been doing with my useless body-surf tactics. I followed suit! We rolled and rolled until finally we rolled to shore, exhausted. After collapsing and hugging the precious sand, I focused on the saviour still at my side and observed the most incredibly handsome man I had ever seen. Herculean, in fact! 6'5" at least, solid, rippling, bronzed muscle, dark brown hair and beard over a beautiful angular jaw and deep brown eyes that danced with abundant life, a total 'hunk' and, incidentally, the only other living being on the entire beach beside sea gulls. This was worth almost drowning! He was 24, Belgian, and a language major at Monmouth College. His name was Yves. I fell instantly in love! Unfortunately, I found in ensuing conversation, he had a girlfriend. Oh well, so goes life! Girlfriend or no, he was none-the-less my Godsent Angel that day to whom I owe my life and am eternally grateful!

I saw him once more, the following week, same beach, same place, but a nice, sunny beach day. He was accompanied by his friend George and I, my high school buddy, Lana Turner (Honest, that really was her name!) She and George met, dated for a long time and almost married… almost… (Match-making has always been a sideline for me!) After that Sunday, I never saw Yves again.

Three times since my brush with the deep blue, 'THE VOICE' has spoken to me in times of need, always addressing me as "My Beloved Child"… For example, while travelling in Europe in '87 and experiencing a strong sense of isolation and alone-ness, I very audibly heard… *"My Beloved Child, did you think that I would leave you now!"* Wow! My feelings of isolation disappeared instantly and gave way to a joy that brought tears! I'm sure the people around me thought me quite odd! One never knows when an unseen presence might be heard, felt or seen. It can happen anywhere, anytime and to anyone! It is always an awesome experience. I always feel so loved and comforted. I feel and hear the guidance of my angels or guides as I paint, very often, directing my hand, offering suggestions, or whispering colors in my ear. Color is always offered up in one word… Blue! Green! Red!… etc. They're very emphatic about color, and they're usually right.

We all receive guidance, help and nurturing from the unseen realms; we just don't always listen or pay attention. Whatever may seemingly be, we are never alone. This I know.

In '86 I met my soul-mate, finally! We were married 5 months later and have lived happily ever after, first in Laguna Beach, CA, and since June of '96 on the gorgeous Monterey Peninsula. Al McDaniel is a retired test pilot whose thrilling career in aviation spanned half a century. Hired by Hughes Aircraft Co. in '49 by 'The Man'- Howard Hughes himself, he really got to live his dream. Now we live our dream together! We give thanks every day for each other, the deep love we share and all the blessings bestowed upon us in this life. We work hard at everything we undertake and usually undertake too much! That creative drive just doesn't recognize boundaries or limitations. All my life I have defied limitation. I don't believe God placed any of us here to live a limited, boring life… Jesus tells us HE came so that we might have life and have it more abundantly! A magnificent promise I take quite literally!

Make creative, abundant life your goal. Accept nothing less! Remember love is always the answer! Love Mother Earth, love others, love the critters, love yourself! Remember you are a Beloved Child of God. Take time to nurture yourself. Smile more, laugh more, worry less! Enjoy this life, this precious gift… the miracle has occurred, YOU ARE! CELEBRATE! May you be abundantly blessed as you continue on your path and the Angels envelope you in love every step of the way.

In Dreams

We will only have peace on Earth
when the day comes we can dance with
one another without stepping
on each other's feet.